# The Mystery of
# Mr. Nice

FROM THE TATTERED CASEBOOK OF

**CHET GECKO**
PRIVATE EYE

*Bruce Hale*

HARCOURT, INC.

*San Diego • New York • London*

Requests for permission to make copies of any part
of the work should be mailed to the following address:
Permissions Department, Harcourt, Inc.,
6277 Sea Harbor Drive, Orlando, Florida 32887-6777

www.harcourt.com

First Harcourt paperbacks edition 2001
First published 2000

The Library of Congress has cataloged the hardcover edition as follows:
Hale, Bruce.
The mystery of Mr. Nice: from the tattered casebook of Chet Gecko,
private eye/written and illustrated by Bruce Hale.
p. cm.
"A Chet Gecko Mystery."
Summary: When the principal of his school begins
acting nice to him, Chet Gecko realizes that he is an imposter
and so sets out to find the real one.
[1. Geckos—Fiction.  2. Lizards—Fiction.  3. Schools—Fiction.
4. Mystery and detective stories.]  I. Title.
PZ7.H1295My   2000
[Fic]—dc21      99-50914
ISBN 0-15-202271-6
ISBN 0-15-202515-4 pb

Text set in Bembo
Display type set in Elroy
Designed by Ivan Holmes

E G H F

Printed in the United States of America

For my brother, the one and only Matteo Grande

# The Mystery of
# Mr. Nice

**A private message from the private eye . . .**

Nobody appreciates great artists when they're still alive.

Take that Vincent van Gogh guy, for example. He chopped off his ear because nobody liked his art. That must have hurt. Both the lack of respect and the ear chopping, I mean.

But I know how he felt.

How do I know? I'm another unsung artist.

True, most folks know me as the best lizard detective at Emerson Hicky Elementary, but it's not all knuckles and know-how with Chet Gecko. I've also got my artistic side.

And if it wasn't for my art, I might never have stumbled over the clue that started me on this case.

Don't get me wrong. I'm not going to quit detective work and chop off my ear anytime soon. (Geckos don't have ears.) But I wouldn't mind a little more respect for my talents.

After all, who do you think put the *art* in *smart aleck*?

# 1

## Wombat Kisses

It was a hot, slow day. History class crept by like a slug on ice. Mr. Ratnose stood at the blackboard, trying to make some history of his own as Most Boring Teacher Ever. Half the class was asleep, and the other half was trying to look like they weren't.

Me, I was watching Mr. Ratnose's long whiskers droop like the seat of a kindergartner's pj's.

Suddenly, inspiration struck.

I whipped out a sheet of paper and a pen. Behind the cover of my open history book, I began a truly great cartoon. It started with Mr. Ratnose, and for the sake of Art, I made his nose four times the size it usually is.

And that's pretty big.

Then I pooched out his lips. With great detail, I drew in Marge Supial, the school nurse, puckering up for the mother of all kisses.

Before I'd even finished, I heard a smothered giggle. I glanced over at Bo Newt.

"Eeew, wombat kisses!" he whispered.

He giggled some more. Shirley Chameleon scooted her desk closer, trying to see what all the fuss was about.

"*Shhh,*" I said. An artist must have silence. I bent to my work. I had just labeled the characters in my latest masterpiece, when IT fell on me.

The teacher's shadow.

"What do you call *this*?" said Mr. Ratnose.

"Um . . . art gecko?" I said.

"And who is that supposed to be?" He pointed a clawed finger at the big-nosed rat.

Duh. It was obviously him. But I couldn't say that.

"Um, it's an Afro-Cubist rendering of a rare lumpenhuffer in a Post Toasties–influenced style," I said. That's the kind of stuff I read in my parents' art books at home. No fooling.

"It looks like me kissing a wombat," said Mr. Ratnose. He bared his long front teeth.

The kids sitting near me were trying so hard not to crack up, they were snorting like pigs at a mud festival. Bo Newt's eyes bulged like two pumped-up grapefruit. He clapped a hand over his mouth.

My lip twitched into a semi-smirk. I couldn't help it.

"You think that's funny?" said Mr. Ratnose.

"No, I think it's art," I said.

My public agreed. I could tell because smothered laughter was turning their faces as purple as a grape-stomper's socks.

Mr. Ratnose frowned. His ears quivered. "Well, I think it's awful," he said, grabbing my drawing. "It shows a lack of respect."

Everybody's an art critic.

Mr. Ratnose scribbled on his pink pad. He tore off the sheet and thrust it at me. Then he ripped my sketch in half.

*Ouch.* That hurt. But every great artist suffers insults in his time. I knew that future art lovers would recognize my genius.

"Chet Gecko," said Mr. Ratnose, "go straight to the principal's office, and take this–this *thing*." He pointed at my mangled artwork. "Mr. Zero will deal with you!"

He stalked back to the front of the room, hairless tail dragging behind him.

I sighed and got up to go. An artist's life is not an easy one. That's why I usually stick with detecting.

People might make fun of my detective work, but they can't tear it up.

As I walked down the aisle, a bird's voice chirped, "Mr. Ratnose, Chet's not taking the drawing with him."

I glanced over at her. Cassandra the Stool Pigeon. It figured.

I went back and picked up my drawing, then trudged out the door and down the hall.

Some days are like that. They begin with a punch to the gut or a mud pie in the kisser. You figure when a day starts like that, things can't get much worse.

But then, somehow or other, they do.

# 2

## Ground Zero

Visiting Principal Zero's office is about as much fun as going to a hungry shark's birthday party. You never know whether you're a guest or the dessert.

Principal Zero and I had tangled in the past. He was the fattest of fat cats with the meanest of tempers. Big Fat Zero, the kids called him—but never to his face.

Principal Zero was the kind of guy who would stuff your mouth full of tardy slips, then paddle your behind for mumbling. He liked art about as much as Mr. Ratnose did.

I was doomed.

As I approached the principal's office, my heart beat like a hyperactive octopus with a drum set. I wasn't nervous, exactly. I just liked having some skin left on my tuckus.

His secretary, a crow named Maggie with a voice like sandpaper, sat polishing her beak at her desk. I stopped to talk.

"Hey, brown eyes," I said. "How's tricks?"

"Stuff the sweet talk," she said. "You're in trouble, or you wouldn't be here."

"Right as rain," I said. Can't fool a secretary. "Is your boss in?"

Maggie ruffled her feathers. "Just your luck; he is."

I looked around the waiting room. Strange. Where a line of smart alecks usually sat waiting for justice, empty chairs greeted me.

*Principal Zero must have his punishment on speed dial,* I thought.

"Go right in," said Maggie.

That crazy octopus in my chest played another drum solo. This time, he did a rim shot on my stomach.

I took a deep breath and stepped inside. Behind a broad black desk sat Principal Zero, the source of all discipline at Emerson Hicky Elementary. I knew I was about to get mine.

Principal Zero's claws flexed, and his tail twitched. His wide smile was as full of poison as a cobra's toothbrush. "Yes?" he said.

I laid my pink slip and torn drawing side by side on his desk. He looked from one to the other. I studied the desktop.

"Nice artwork, Mr. . . . Gecko," he said.

I looked up again.

Principal Zero was giving himself a dignified tongue bath. "It has a wonderful sense of color, and the style is quite—how should I put this?—quite mature," he said.

I blinked. He was serious.

"Lovely use of dark and light," said Principal Zero. He picked up the pink slip. "Now, what seems to be the problem?"

"Well, Mr. Ratnose didn't . . . um . . . like my drawing."

"How strange," he said. "Perhaps his taste in art is not so refined. I'd love a piece like this for my collection. Could you bear to part with it?"

That's when I knew.

Either my principal had lost his mind, or someone had kidnapped the real Mr. Zero.

# 3

## Unprincipaled Behavior

**S**urprise froze my tongue like a mayfly on a Popsicle. I couldn't believe what was happening.

"So, may I keep this wonderful drawing?" asked Principal Zero again.

"Uh ... sure," I said. "It's yours."

He glanced down at the pink slip.

"Thank you ... Chet." Mr. Zero's smile was as sincere as a bully's apology. "Be sure to stop in anytime. I'm always glad to see an artist of your amazing talents."

I nodded and stumbled from the room, breathless and bewildered. I shut his door and leaned against it. Maggie Crow was riffling through a file drawer with her beak.

I cleared my throat. "Notice anything strange about your boss?"

"No stranger than usual," she said.

"But he didn't punish me."

Maggie turned and cocked her head. "Maybe you caught him in a good mood. Don't push your luck, buddy-boy. Get out while the getting's good."

I beat feet. My mind was racing like a kid after an ice-cream truck. Something truly weird was going on here.

And I was just the gecko to find out what it was.

At recess, I plopped down under a scrofulous tree to think. Questions chased each other like third graders playing a game of cooties. I was so distracted, I barely tasted my Pillbug Crunch candy bar.

If that really *was* Principal Zero, why was he acting so . . . well, *nice*? If that wasn't my principal, who was it, and why was he pretending?

And what the heck was a hypotenuse, anyway? (I hadn't read my math homework again.)

I looked up. Across the playground, Rocky Rhode, the horned toad, was holding a first grader upside down until lunch money rained from his pockets. The old shakedown.

I shook my head. That sixth-grade troublemaker was guilty of everything from stealing test answers to writing graffiti on a sleeping teacher. She was bad news with a capital *B*.

*Hmm.* Maybe I could try the old shakedown on *her.* Rocky spent more time in the principal's office than his secretary did. She might have a clue about why our principal was acting strange.

I strolled across the grass as Rocky dropped the little shrew on his head. He staggered off, whimpering.

"Hey, Rocky," I said.

She squinted up at me as she collected the fallen coins. "Hello, Gecko," she sneered. "Looking for trouble?"

"No, thanks," I said. "I've got plenty. What I need is answers."

"Can you pay?"

"I might."

Rocky looked both ways. No teachers nearby. "Which test did you want the answers to?" she said.

She dug a fistful of papers from her book bag.

I snatched one and scooted back. "No test answers for me," I said. "I want a different kind of answer. And if I don't get it, I'm going straight to the principal with this."

I expected her to take a stab at rearranging my face with her horned fists. I was wrong.

"Hah!" she laughed. "That's a good one! Principal Zero would probably give me a gold star."

My jaw hung open. "So you've noticed that he's ... different?"

Rocky snorted. "Different? He changed like magic."

Magic?

An idea came to me. That happens sometimes.

"Rocky," I said, "do you know if Principal Zero has ever been involved with voodoo?"

"Who do?"

"No, voodoo."

"Zero, voodoo? Sure, I do."

"You do?"

"Yeah," she said. "And the answer is no. But *something's* happened to him."

I sighed and handed back the test sheet. "Here, I don't need this."

Rocky stuffed it back into her book bag, which was jammed with papers, stolen lunch money, and what looked like a very cramped kindergartner. I shoved my hands in my pockets and turned to go.

"Hey, Gecko," said Rocky. "I'll give you one answer for free. You wanna know how different Zero is?"

I turned to face her. "Yeah."

"Yesterday, Teach sent me to the principal's office for swiping lunch money from someone's desk. But all Zero said was, 'Next time, don't get caught.'"

Rocky shrugged a spiky shoulder. "He told me he'd help me practice my technique. Now, that's what I call a nice principal."

Things were worse than I thought. I had to act fast.

"See ya around, Rocky." I turned and started across the playground.

"Hey, answer *me* something," Rocky shouted after me. "Why don't burglars make good actors? . . . Give up? Because they always try to steal the show!"

I shook my head and walked on.

She should know better. Comedy and crime just don't mix.

# 4

# A Chirp Off the Old Block

I walked across the grass, working things over in my mind. My keen detective instincts told me something was seriously screwy.

A shadow fell across me. I ducked.

"Hey, Chet!"

I looked up. It was only Natalie Attired, my partner. She floated down and made a neat two-point landing on a low branch. Mockingbirds have some serious moves.

"I just heard a great joke," she said. "What's the difference between a teacher and a train?"

"Huh?"

"A teacher says, 'Spit out your gum,' and a train says, 'Chew, chew, chew.'" She cackled. "Pretty good, eh?"

"A riot," I said.

"What's the matter, Chet? Got a bug stuck in your craw?"

"Nope, a mystery."

I told her about my strange meeting with Principal Zero and what Rocky had said.

"Yeah, so?" said Natalie. "Maybe he got a personality transplant—they dumped his, and put in the personality of someone nice."

She laughed.

"You laugh," I said, "but nobody could change that fast. And even if he could, why would he start being nice to *me*? That's not our principal in there."

"So?"

I paced on the grass. "So, bird-brain, the principal is only the most powerful guy in the school. If someone has kidnapped Mr. Zero and substituted an impostor, that's scary. Who knows what they might be planning?"

We both fell silent. Natalie groomed her feathers thoughtfully.

"But you don't know for *sure* that someone switched principals on us," she said. "He could just be in a good mood."

We looked at each other.

"Nah," we said together. Mr. Zero hadn't had a good mood since the *Titanic* was just a dinghy.

"I've got a nose for danger," I said, "and I tell you something's rotten here."

"You've got a nose for sweet snacks and deep-fried termites," she said. "But you have been known to sniff out a mystery now and then...with my help."

"Hah! You're lucky I *let* you help. Without me, you'd spend your time counting worms, doing homework—"

"And getting better grades," she said. "So, if we're going to unravel the mystery of Mr. Nice, where do we start?"

I munched my Pillbug Crunch bar. We chewed over some ideas.

"We could try following him around," I said. "He might do something to give himself away."

"But how will we get out of class?"

Oh yeah. Class. It sure got in the way of detective work.

"I know!" she said. "Let's search his office. Maybe we can find a clue."

"Now you're talking, tootsie!"

" 'Tootsie'?"

"Hey, that's what they say in detective movies," I said.

We needed a plan. After all, Maggie Crow wouldn't just let us waltz in and search her boss's office. And Principal Zero (or whoever he was) probably wouldn't roll out the welcome mat and serve us tea and cookies, either.

We needed something to get them out of the office for a while. A diversion. *Hmmm.*

"Tell me," I said, "are the Newt Brothers still taking karate lessons?"

"I think so," said Natalie.

"Have them join us, chop-chop. We'll meet behind the cafeteria at lunchtime. Mrs. Crow will be in the teachers' lunchroom, and I think I know how to get the principal out of his office."

"Roger," she said.

"'Roger?' I'm Chet."

Natalie shrugged. "Hey, that's what they say in detective movies."

That Natalie. What a joker.

The bell rang. We headed back to class. With a bit of luck, lunchtime would bring the answer to our question: Had our principal gone plumb crazy, or was he off somewhere taking the Big Nap?

# 5

# Everybody Was Kung-Food Fighting

The lunch bell jangled. I strolled with the other kids to the cafeteria—my favorite place on campus. My steps slowed as I passed the trays of steaming delicacies. But I had no time for Mystery Meat or Chef's Surprise.

Chet Gecko was on the case.

Natalie and the Newt Brothers were waiting outside. We watched the main office until Mrs. Crow left for lunch, bob-bob-bobbin' along toward a juicy worm, no doubt. Yuck. A janitor followed her, pushing a cart.

That left only Principal Zero inside.

I turned to Bo and Tony Newt.

"Okay, boys. Make it good. You've got to keep him away from the office for at least five minutes."

"No problem-o, Chet," said Bo. He grinned from ear to ear, like Peter Pumpkin Eater at a jack-o'-lantern convention.

"Yeah," said Tony, hooking a thumb toward his brother. "I'm gonna love creaming this creep."

"Who you calling a creep, you moth-brain?" Bo aimed a kick at his brother's head.

Tony ducked and karate-chopped back. They burst through the cafeteria doors faster than a vice principal after a sassy eighth grader.

Tony snatched a chunk of mealworm casserole off some kid's tray.

"Yoohoo, bug-breath!" He tossed the food at his brother's face. Bo ducked, and the gooey mess splatted onto a fat toad at the next bench.

I sighed. It was a shame to waste chow, but desperate times called for desperate measures.

"Nice shot, booger-brain," said Bo. "Take *that*!"

He flung a lump of Jell-O at Tony. Tony dodged, and the gelatin ploshed into the lap of one of the Rat Sisters. She growled and hefted her soup bowl.

"FOOD FIGHT!" I screamed.

The cafeteria erupted in airborne edibles. Casserole and Jell-O flew through the air with the greatest of cheese. Rolls bounced, doughnuts danced, and salad got undressed. It looked like a family of cross-eyed jugglers had gone berserk in a deli.

I wanted to stay and help clean up the leftovers,

21

but lunch would have to wait. Natalie tugged me out the door. "Come *on*," she said.

We stopped outside the principal's office and ducked behind the bushes.

"Watch this mockingbird go to work," said Natalie. She buzzed like an office intercom.

"Principal Zero, come quick!" said Natalie in Maggie Crow's voice. "There's a food fight in the cafeteria!"

Whoever he was, he still acted like a principal. The huge cat staggered out the door, tugging on some loose skin at his neck, waddling off as fast as he could go.

"Oh, the waste!" moaned Principal Zero.

I smirked. "He has quite a waist himself."

Natalie eyed my belly. "You should talk, Mr. Can't-Say-No-to-a-Pillbug-Crunch-Bar."

"Hey, at least I don't have worm-breath," I said. I narrowed my eyes. "Now, you want to swap insults or search this joint?"

We searched the joint. Natalie checked the principal's file cabinets and corkboard. I took his desk.

"What are we looking for, anyway?" she said.

"Anything that can give us the lowdown. Medical records, ransom notes, maps to secret hideouts—anything at all."

I looked in the wastebasket. It was empty as a vampire's vanity mirror.

I sifted through the papers on the desk. Report cards overflowed his in-box. When I saw my own, I paused. A C+ in English? Just because I told the teacher that Shakespeare was an old English javelin thrower?

School wasn't fair.

I moved on. A hefty book, *Crime and Punishment in Primary School,* sat open on his desk. A half-eaten fish-gut sandwich pinned down a stack of old homework papers and drawings. I noticed my own masterpiece among them.

A "private collection," eh?

"Hey, Chet, look at this," said Natalie.

She held up a calendar. On it, Friday's date was circled in red. *PTA meeting* was scrawled in the same color.

"Do you think it means something?" she said.

"Yeah. It means he's going to the PTA meeting. Anything else?"

Natalie shook her head and turned back to the file cabinet. I slid open a desk drawer. A well-worn copy of *Advanced Spanking Techniques* rested on some rolled-up papers.

I unrolled one batch. It looked like floor plans for buildings. The top of each sheet read, *Vocational School*.

Since when was Principal Zero an architect?

"Check this out," I said.

"Yes?" A deep voice answered.

*Uh-oh.* The principal's huge body filled the doorway. His tail twitched like a snake doing the jitterbug.

"What are you doing here?" growled Big Fat Zero.

I glanced around the room. "Oh. Uh . . . the sunlamp. We came here to work on our tans."

His eyes narrowed. "What sunlamp? This is an office."

"I was misinformed," I said.

I stuffed the drawings back into his drawer. Natalie dropped a file folder and joined me by the desk.

"Anything else?" said Principal Zero.

"Yeah," I said. I pointed to the building plans. "Do you know what *vocational* means?"

"It means 'relating to training for a job or career,'" he said.

"Thanks," I said. "I was wondering."

Principal Zero stepped toward us. His lip curled in a snarl. Then . . .

"Thanks for keeping an eye on the office while I was gone," he said. His sudden smile was as transparent as a good deed on report-card day. "You're such helpful students. Would you like some dessert?"

He held out a tray of pudding—butterscotch, with big, juicy carpenter ants inside. My mouth watered. I reached for the tray.

"Ow!"

Natalie had stomped on my foot. I glared at her. She smiled.

"Oops," she said. "Lost my balance. Isn't it time for us to go, Chet?"

"Huh? Oh . . . yeah," I grumbled. "Thanks anyway, Mr. Zero. See you around."

He stepped aside to let us pass. As I looked up at Principal Zero, I noticed an odd line on his neck, almost like a scar. His phony smile stretched wider than a hippo's hammock.

"Come back anytime, children." He purred. "My door is always open."

When we were out of earshot, Natalie spoke.

"What was the big idea, taking pudding from him?"

"Why not?" I said. My taste buds hadn't forgiven her yet.

"It was a bribe, you dingdong. He was trying to throw you off track. You were right, Chet—there *is* something fishy going on."

"You think so?"

"He's as phony as your book report on *The Wonders of Plankton*."

I winced. "Hey, I'll have you know it took me a long time to make up that book."

I led the way into the cafeteria. Most of the food was back where it belonged, on trays or in kids' mouths. Lunchroom monitors were mopping up the rest.

I grabbed a tray.

"Wait a minute," said Natalie. "Don't you want to talk about this?"

"After lunch, partner. I do my best thinking on a full stomach."

I piled on the Mystery Meat.

Something was rotten at Emerson Hicky Elementary. That fake principal was dealing dirty at my school, and the whole setup stank like a sweat-sock soufflé.

Or maybe that was just the cafeteria casserole.

Either way, Chet Gecko had a full plate of detective work. And it was time to dig in.

# 6

## Hamster Is as Hamster Does

By the time we finished eating, Natalie and I had planned our next moves. She would fake being sick, which wasn't too hard, given the casserole. While visiting Marge Supial, the nurse, Natalie would listen in on the principal's office next door.

I decided to track down Principal Zero's garbage. A man's garbage can tell you a lot about him. Like what kind of candy bars he eats, or what work he does, or whether he's been doing a little kidnapping lately.

With luck, I might catch the janitor with Principal Zero's trash still in his cart. The clock showed ten minutes left in lunch period. Natalie and I split on our separate missions.

"Meet you after school by the flagpole," I said. "Make sure you're not followed."

Natalie winked at me and began staggering toward the lunch monitors.

"Oooh, I don't feel so good." She moaned like a movie star in search of an Oscar. "Everything's getting hazy."

That Natalie. What an actress.

I hotfooted it for the janitor's office. I didn't relish digging through huge bins of spoiled food to find Principal Zero's trash. I hoped the janitor's cart was still there.

Luck was with me.

I walked up to the cart and reached into the plastic trash barrel. Garbage from two buildings' worth of wastebaskets greeted me. This wasn't going to be easy. I started looking for telltale candy wrappers.

Like me, the principal is a man of big appetites.

I was up to my elbows in English papers when I heard a foot scuff on the pavement. I turned.

"Looking for something?" said a shifty-eyed hamster with a stubbly beard. He was wearing a pair of greasy blue overalls that said GUIDO on the left front pocket.

I pushed my hat back on my head and let my eyes go as dull as a lawn mower in a rock garden.

"Um, yeah. I'm like, y'know, looking for a paper

I lost, y'know? Would you find a janitor to help me look?" (Natalie wasn't the only one who could act.)

"I'm a janitor," said the hamster.

I gave him the once-over.

The hamster was a big guy. But no wider than a cement mixer and no taller than a stack of sabertooth tigers. A pair of brass knuckles twinkled merrily from the breast pocket of his overalls.

If he was a janitor, I was the Easter Gecko.

"Cool," I said. "You must be a new janitor, Mr. . . . Guido?"

He scratched at his whiskers with a meaty paw. "Just started this week," he said.

"Like, can you help me find my report? I think I left it in the principal's office and he, y'know, tossed it."

"Ya want me to root through that trash with ya?"

"Like, totally."

Guido squinted at me for a long moment. I grinned like I didn't have a thought in my head. It wasn't too hard.

"Okay, I'll show ya where to look," he said. "But make it snappy." Guido pointed to a corner of the trash barrel with a finger like a spear. "I dumped the boss—er, the principal's stuff over there."

"Like, thanks, dude. For sure."

I rummaged through the trash in a hurry. I

couldn't talk this way much longer without losing a few IQ points.

Guido leaned on a nearby box, picking his buck-teeth with a file and watching me. I didn't find the candy wrappers I'd expected. I did find dull reports, equipment lists, soggy dynamite, escape routes for getaway cars. . . .

Wait a minute.

It was pretty odd stuff to find in Principal Zero's trash. But then, he was a pretty odd principal. I shook my head.

"Come on, kid," said Guido. "Hurry it up."

The hamster stood and started pacing. He bounced the file lightly against his thick paw.

My time was running short. I dug deeper. And then I saw something.

A list scribbled in dark pen strokes:

> *Pocket picking*
> *Robbery*
> *Grand theft auto*
> *Spelling*
> *Advanced lying*
> *Assault and battery*

"Whatcha got there, kid?" said the fake janitor. He leaned over the trash barrel and reached for the list.

I snatched the paper and jammed it into my pocket.

"Totally radical!" I said. "I found it, dude. Like, thanks so much."

His heavy paw fell on my shoulder. "Let's see it, bright boy. Gotta make sure it's yours. Can't have someone taking trash what don't belong to 'em."

I searched my mind for ideas. But it was as empty as a school locker in summertime. My tail curled.

He stuck out his other paw, demanding.

*Rrrring!*

I was never so glad to hear a phone ring. The hamster's eyes shifted toward a black telephone on the desk.

"Don't move," he said. He went to answer the ringing phone. I scooted out the door as I heard him say, "Yeah? Oh, yes, sir!"

I trotted off to class as the school bell sounded. If that janitor had been any more attached to his garbage, there'd be a trash-can wedding on the way. Strange.

I dropped into my seat, then pulled out the list and scanned it again.

What did it mean? It didn't look like any shopping list I'd ever seen. If the fake principal was up to something, I'd have bet my allowance that this new janitor was in on it, too.

That made me wonder: Who else at Emerson Hicky was cooking up fiendish plans?

"Chet Gecko, come up here and answer the questions from last night's math homework."

Who else besides my teacher, I meant.

# 7

## Talking Trash with Ms. DeBree

**M**ath class limped by. English class crawled. If my classes got any slower, they'd roll over and croak like a toad.

I started to wonder why I was so eager to solve the mystery of Principal Zero. I mean, even if he was an impostor, could school possibly get any worse?

I shuddered. I didn't want to know the answer to that question. I would solve the mystery because I was a detective, and that's what detectives do.

"Hey, Chet," Bo Newt whispered.

"Yo, Bo," I whispered back.

"Lunchtime was fun," he said. "When can I do more detective work?"

"Stay tuned. If things start cracking, I'll let you know."

"Cool," he said.

You know times are tough when your best backup is a newt.

When the school bell rang, we all blasted out the door like milk spray after a bad joke. I approached the bushes where I stash my skateboard.

A chill of suspicion tickled my spine. I paused and eyeballed everyone passing by. How many of these smiling faces were in on the principal's plot? How many students, and how many teachers?

I fished out my skateboard and went rolling into the great unknown.

*Ouch!*

It turned out to be a slow second grader. After brushing myself off and muttering a quick apology, I headed for the flagpole and my meeting with Natalie.

Then it hit me: I knew what we had to do. But we'd have to hurry.

Natalie was waiting. "Hiya, Chet. You'll never guess what I found out."

"Save it, birdie. We've got business that can't wait." I crooked my finger at her. "Come on."

I rolled back down the halls to the janitor's office, with Natalie floating close behind. I told her about my meeting with Guido.

She flapped her wings lazily. "Sounds like a tough customer. So, why do you want to talk to him again?"

"Not him, his supervisor."

Ms. Maureen DeBree was the head custodian. Not a banana peel fell at Emerson Hicky that she didn't know about. She'd have the lowdown on the new janitor, and maybe even know a thing or two about the fake Mr. Zero.

I rapped on her door. "Ms. DeBree? It's Chet Gecko. Are you there?"

The door swung open. Standing tall like a totem pole of ugliness was Guido the Hamster. His buckteeth gleamed in a mean grin.

"Well, if it ain't the snoopy gecko," he said. "What brings ya back, sniffin' around here?"

"We're looking for Ms. DeBree," said Natalie.

Guido made a sound like a salamander swallowing a shoehorn. I guess he was laughing.

"Well, yer lookin' in the wrong place, ya Nosy Nellies," said Guido. "She's home sick all week. I'm in charge here." He stabbed his chest with a thick thumb. Even his knuckles had muscles on them.

I looked up at him. Guido wasn't the brightest bulb on the marquee. Maybe we could draw a little information out of him on the sly.

"So, tell me, Mr. Guido," I said, "where do you know Mr. Zero from?"

"From upstate," said Guido. He scratched his belly. "Me and him did time—uh, spent time together awhile back."

Natalie picked up the ball. "Oh, you worked together?"

"Yeah, we done plenty of jobs together," he said. Guido scratched behind his ear. It was either fleas or soap rash. I was betting on fleas.

"I see," I said. "And when was this—last year, the year before?"

"Yeah, last ye—" His eyes narrowed. "Hey, what's with the third degree here?"

"Just curious," I said. "I was wondering how Principal Zero could have worked with you last year when he's been here at Emerson Hicky since I was in kindergarten."

At last somebody hit the On switch in his brain. Guido clenched his fists and snarled.

"Scram, ya nosy little brats! Or I'll moidlerize ya!"

We scrammed. You didn't need a Criminal-English dictionary to guess that *moidlerizing* would be bad for your health.

As Natalie and I reached the school gate, she saluted me with a wing feather.

"Nice work, private eye," she said. "Looks like they're in it together. Let's meet at your place in an hour, and I'll tell you what I heard in the nurse's office."

"Wait," I said. "Where are you going?"

"Home to do my homework," she said. "You might try it sometime."

"Hah!" I snorted. "Homework is for sissies."

But I'd never let my mom hear me say that.

Natalie shook her head. "See you in an hour," she said.

Natalie took off. I rolled past the students and teachers leaving school. My radar was up. Every teacher's frown set my nerves on edge. Even the crossing guards looked cross.

Just before my house, I slowed to turn into the driveway.

And then it came.

*"Yaaah!"*

A dark shape lunged from a bush. It knocked me off the skateboard. We tumbled onto the grass.

As we rolled, I pinned my attacker to the ground.

"Hah!" I shouted. "Got you, you—Pinky?"

My little sister squirmed under me.

"Get off!" she said. "I'm telling Mom."

"That's rich, coming from you," I said. "*You're* the one who ambushed *me.*"

I've matched wits with king cobras and tangled with Gila monsters. Not many foes could make this private eye lose his cool.

My sister could.

"Okay, roach-breath, I'll let you up," I said. "Stop bucking."

She stopped. We glared at each other, then stood and brushed ourselves off.

"I swear, Pinky, you'd make a great criminal mastermind, given half a chance."

Pinky planted her hands on her hips. "Unh-uh!" she said, shaking her head. "Yesterday, the prince-apo' came to our class, an' he said I'd make a rotten crinimal."

I leaned forward. "What?"

She stuck her chest out. "Yeah. Prince-apo' Zero asked who thinks it's okay to lie an' steal. Some kids raised their hands. But *I* told him it's wrong."

"And what did he do?"

"Wrote down the kids' names who raised their hands."

I shook my head. Stranger and stranger.

"Thanks, Pinky," I said.

She ducked her head, shy as a goose at a barnyard boogie night. "For what?" she said.

Pinky headed for the front door.

I strolled into the backyard. Time to hit the office for some serious brainwork.

"Chet!" My mom stood in the back doorway, arms crossed. "Do you have any homework today?"

Oops. Not the kind of brainwork I had in mind.

"Oh, uh...not much," I said.

"Well, make sure you do it before dinner..."

Suggestions didn't work with me.

"Or no dessert for you," she said.

Threats did.

"Okay, mom. In a minute." I waded through the tall grass toward my own private think tank.

My office sits up against the fence, behind a clump of bamboo. It's cleverly disguised as a big re-frigerator box. On one side, I have a Saran Wrap window with my name on it, just like the big-shot detectives have.

The little details make all the difference.

I crawled inside. I sat thinking about the case and reading my name on the window: OꓘƆƎ⅁ ⅂ƎHƆ. I hoped that when Natalie showed up, she'd bring some hot clues.

Or at least some hot cocoa. I was hungry again.

From my emergency stash, I pulled out a Three Mosquitoes candy bar. Small, but tasty. I got out my crayons and started sketching a new comic book.

Sometimes drawing relaxes me and helps me think about the case I'm on.

Not this time. I drew big-muscled hamsters and kindergartners in prison clothes.

This case had me in a grip tighter than a turtle's underwear.

I had just started looking for another candy bar when I heard leaves crunching outside.

Footsteps. I reached for my trusty rubber-band gun and held my breath.

# 8

## The Plot Sickens

"Who's there?" I said.

"Get your tail out here right now, young Gecko," said a voice that sounded like Principal Zero's.

I pulled back the rubber band. "Wh-what?"

"Gotcha! Chet, it's me, Natalie," said a voice that sounded like Natalie's. You can never be sure with a mockingbird.

"What's the secret password?" I said.

"Come on, Chet, let me in. I brought grass-hopper cookies and cocoa."

"Close enough," I said. "Come in."

We got settled, had our snack, and talked about the case. I told Natalie what I'd just learned from Pinky and showed her the mysterious list I'd found in the trash.

"Maybe it's some kind of to-do list," she said.

"If that's the case, some crook's going to be busier than a bunny at an all-you-can-eat salad bar. But why did they include *spelling*?"

Natalie shrugged. "Beats me. But, hey, guess what I overheard at the nurse's office. The principal had two visitors. I didn't recognize their voices."

"What did they say?"

"Something about the PTA meeting. Then one of them asked, 'Is he still under wraps?' And the principal said, 'Yeah, he won't give us any trouble.'"

I drained the cup of cocoa and wiped off my chocolate mustache. "Anything else?" I said.

"Just this," said Natalie. "I poked around in back of the nurse's office, where they keep the extra school supplies. And I found a big box of brass knuckles."

"*Hmm*...reading and writing and rhythmic hits," I said. I paced back and forth, and bumped into the side of the box. I needed a bigger office. Or a smaller partner.

"Natalie, anyone at school could be in on this plot."

"Anyone?" she said. "Isn't that a bit much?"

"Okay, maybe just half the school," I said.

Natalie snorted. "Come on, Chet. Think about it. Principal Zero just got weird this week, right?"

"Right."

"And that phony janitor said *he* started work this week."

"Yeah, so?"

"So, maybe we should check out any teachers or students who just came to Emerson Hicky."

She was pretty smart. For a bird.

"Let's start tomorrow," I said. "I have a hunch that we'd better solve this case before that PTA meeting on Friday. Something's going to happen there."

"Then let's start tonight," she said.

"Why?"

"Tomorrow's Friday, Chet."

Details. They'll get you every time.

"Okay," I said, "we'll start right away. Let's—"

"Chet!" called my mother. "Dinnertime! And don't forget to do your homework afterward."

"Okay, Mom!"

Natalie smirked. "Looks like you have more important business," she said. "'Only sissies do homework,' eh?"

"Ha, ha," I said. "I'll meet you tomorrow before school. We'll see what the early bird catches."

"Chet, come in right now!" my mom shouted. "I'm not going to call you again."

I went into the house. Mysteries are like meat and drink to a detective. But sometimes there's just no substitute for Mom's mothloaf smothered in gravy.

45

# 9

## Armadillo Dallying

**E**arly the next morning, a rosy glaze covered the sky and dew sparkled on the grass as I left for school. At least I think it did. A rosy glaze covered my eyeballs, too.

I hate mornings.

Natalie waited by the cafeteria, whistling a happy tune and twirling a worm. Birds.

"Hiya, Chet," she said. "Ready for some first-class snooping?"

"Ready to go back to bed and sleep until lunch." I yawned.

"Come on. Let's catch some bad guys while they're still groggy."

I grunted and led the way to the principal's office. Maggie Crow was another early bird. She could

tell us who was new at Emerson Hicky and point us toward some suspects.

If she wanted to.

Natalie and I stopped in at Mrs. Crow's desk.

"He's not here yet, kids," she said. "You're going to have to wait for the Paddle of Doom."

"We came to see you, sugar-beak," I said. "Not your boss."

"Yeah?" said Maggie Crow skeptically. She groomed her wing feathers. "What about?"

I glanced at Natalie. I hadn't figured out that part yet. "Umm...," I said.

Natalie took a sneaky approach. "Oh, Mrs.

Crow," she said, "we're forming a Welcome Wagon. Chet and I want to welcome the new students and teachers here, make them feel at home."

"Why, that's a lovely idea," said Maggie Crow. She beamed at Natalie.

Sucker.

"We figured we'd start with the ones who just came this week," I said. "Can you tell us who they are?"

Maggie Crow leaned back in her chair and snagged a file from the stack on the filing cabinet. She paged through it.

"Yep, here we go," she said. "There are only four newcomers: Guido the janitor; Mr. Clint Squint, the vice principal; a sixth-grade teacher, Ms. Echo Darkwing; and a third-grade student named Popper."

We already knew about Guido. That left three suspects to investigate.

"What happened to the old vice principal, Mrs. Shrewer?" said Natalie.

"Funny thing," said Mrs. Crow. "She calls up last Friday, talking in a weird voice. Says she's quitting. Then, out of the blue, this new guy, Mr. Squint, shows up on Monday."

Natalie cocked her head. "Lucky coincidence?" she said.

"You bet," said Maggie Crow.

*Hmm.* Some coincidence. Like it's a coincidence how I show up whenever my mom bakes chocolate-ant cookies. I steered Natalie toward the vice principal's office.

"We'll just go in and welcome Mr. Squint to our happy family," I said. "Have a lovely day."

Mrs. Crow narrowed her eyes suspiciously. Maybe I had laid it on kind of thick.

"Go ahead," she said. "He gets here real early."

I rapped on the vice principal's door. When a gruff voice barked, "What?" I turned the knob.

An armadillo with a bad haircut, Mr. Squint was as short and squat as a bank safe. And his lips were shut just as tightly. He leaned on the edge of his desk, picking his nails with a wicked-looking letter opener.

"Mr. Squint?" I said.

"Who's askin'?" he said.

"We're the Welcome Wagon," said Natalie. "We want to welcome you to our school."

He blinked.

"So . . . welcome," I said.

"Gee. Thanks," said Mr. Squint. He watched us closely with beady black eyes. His ears twitched. Natalie had no more bright ideas, so I put in my two cents.

"Been here long?"

"Not long," he said.

"Where were you before this?"

"Upstate."

"Have you taught class before?"

"Yeah," he said.

Mr. Squint talked like it cost him a dollar for each word. It'd break my piggybank to get a whole speech out of him.

"What did you teach?"

"Boxing," he said. "Why?"

"That's my business," I said.

Mr. Squint stood and flexed. His armor plates bristled.

"I could make your business my business," he said.

"You wouldn't like it," I said. "The pay stinks."

Mr. Squint took a step, and his armored tail knocked a coffee cup off the desk. He bent and reached for it. Suddenly I knew all I needed to know about Mr. Clint Squint.

"Well, it's been swell," I said. "We're off to class."

"Welcome again," said Natalie, "to our happy little home."

"Scat!" he said. We scatted.

Outside the building, Natalie glanced back.

"Why did we leave so fast?" she said.

"Did you see that tattoo on his arm when he

picked up that coffee mug? It had a knife stuck through a heart, and above it, it said PEN STATE."

"So?" she said. "What's Pen State? A writing program?"

"The state prison. Our Mr. Squint is a professional crook."

# 10

# A Froggy Day

We still had ten minutes until school started. Natalie and I headed for the third-grade classroom to check out Popper, the new kid. As we turned the corner, Natalie slowed.

"So, if Mr. Squint's a criminal, what does that have to do with Principal Zero?" she said.

I scratched my chin. "I don't know. But he's probably up to his no-neck in this plot. I'll bet you dollars to doughnuts that Guido the janitor is a crook, too."

"'Dollars to doughnuts'?" said Natalie. She shook her head. "Chet, you say the strangest things."

The doors to the third-grade classroom were locked tighter than a frog's nostril. No lights showed inside.

"Shucks," I said. "Nobody here."

A couple of mice waited outside the door. They were playing the kind of deep and sophisticated game that young rodents love. When one made the other blink, he'd sock his classmate's arm about ten times.

It wasn't chess, but it passed the time.

"Hey," said Natalie. "You kids know where we can find Popper?"

"Poppies?" said the smaller one. A regular Einstein.

"No, dummy," said the bigger one. "They mean Popper, the new kid."

"Oh yeah," said Mouse Einstein. "She likes to hang out at the jungle gym."

He turned to his friend.

"Hey, '*hang out* at the jungle gym.' I made a funny!"

They giggled like a couple of bunnies on a sugar rush. We left them to polish their stand-up comedy act and headed for the playground.

"Chet, that reminds me," said Natalie. "Why was the tuna so sad when he lost his wife?"

I hunched my shoulders. "I have a feeling you're going to tell me," I said.

"He lobster and couldn't flounder! Ha, ha!" Natalie cackled and ruffled her tail feathers.

I groaned.

"Come on, wise up," I said. "Here's the jungle gym, and I bet that's Popper."

Just ahead of us, a brightly striped tree frog was climbing the bars. She wasn't very small—just small enough to fit into a book bag with room left over for books. And she wasn't very energetic—just bouncing around the jungle gym like alien popcorn in a warp-speed popper.

Maybe that's how she got her name. Duh.

"Hey, short stuff," I said. "Are you the one they call Popper?"

"Yup, yup, yup, that's me!" she squeaked.

"We'd like to talk to you," said Natalie.

Popper turned a triple back flip off the highest bar and landed at our feet. She kept vibrating even after she hit the ground.

"Hey, hey, what's up?" she said.

"I'm Chet and this is Natalie. We want to welcome you to our school."

"Hi, hi, hi," said Popper. "You guys are so cool. Better, much better, than the kids at my last school."

Her double-talk was giving me a double headache. Popper twitched and jiggled and quivered like an electric eel in a light socket. If we spent much more time with her, I thought I'd take a socket her myself.

Mornings are not my best time.

"Where were you before this?" I asked.

"Oh, here and there, here and there." She jittered and hopped. "Rotley Elementary, Doofus Junior School, Our Lady of Perpetual Confusion. I move, I move around a lot."

"I hadn't noticed," I said.

"Have you ever been upstate?" asked Natalie.

"Nope, nope, nope. Don't think so."

"Do you know Mr. Squint or Principal Zero?" I said. "And how about a guy named Guido?"

"Nope, nada, zip," she said. "Three strikes, three strikes—that means you're out!"

I gritted my teeth and clenched my fist. Natalie's wing feathers brushed my arm.

"Popper," she said gently, "do you know anything about a vocational school?"

"Hey, hey, hey!" said Popper. "I love vacations, love those vacations."

Natalie sighed. I snarled. The bell rang. No telling what I would've done if it hadn't.

"Bye-bye, you guys, bye-bye!" said Popper. She rocketed off the playground in a green-and-yellow blur.

"Do you really think she's a crook, too?" said Natalie.

I unclenched my jaw. "She's guilty of first-degree babbling and assault with intent to annoy. But those aren't crimes, last time I checked."

"Too bad."

Natalie and I split for class. Popper was a dead end, deader than leftovers from a bullfrog's breakfast. That left Ms. Darkwing, and then we'd be fresh out of leads.

Somehow we had to uncover the plot, find our real principal, and stop the crooks—all before the PTA meeting that evening.

But first, I had an even bigger challenge to tackle. A mean science quiz.

And I hadn't read the homework.

## 11

## Like a Bat Out of Jell-O

At recess I zipped over to Natalie's classroom. We had fifteen minutes to get the scoop on Ms. Darkwing. The Welcome Wagon gag was wearing thin, so I chose a new angle.

"Okay, Natalie," I said, "this time we're reporters for the school newspaper."

"That's news to me," she said.

I sighed. "Come on, let's interview our next suspect."

But when we poked our heads into Ms. Darkwing's classroom, nobody was there. She must have had playground duty.

"We missed her," said Natalie. "What now?"

My eyes roamed the room and settled on the desk. "We snoop."

Ms. Darkwing's desk was so neat, it was scarier than a piggyback ride on a porcupine. All the pencils were sharpened to the same length. All the test papers lined up perfectly.

Spooky.

I squirmed in loathing and slid open a drawer. Natalie peeked over my shoulder.

In flawless order lay a ruler, a lock-picking kit, some brass knuckles, and a stack of papers under a black beanbag-looking thingy with a handle. Natalie picked it up and tapped it on her palm.

"Ow!" she said. "That's some mean beanbag. It wouldn't make much of a beanie creature."

"That's no beanbag, that's a sap."

"No need to get personal. You can be a little ditzy yourself, sometimes."

I gritted my teeth. "Not you, beak-face, *that*— it's a sap."

"A what?"

"A sap." I took it from her and dropped it into my pocket while I sorted through the papers underneath. "Bad guys use them to knock people out."

Natalie raised her eyebrows. "Where do you learn all this stuff, Chet?"

"A detective never reveals his sources," I said. "Hello, what's this?"

I pulled out a sheet of paper. On it, neatly typed, was a familiar list:

*Pocket picking*
*Robbery*
*Grand theft auto*
*Spelling*
*Advanced lying*
*Assault and battery*

It was the same list I'd found in Principal Zero's trash. But it had a tidy new heading on it: *Sixth Grade Class Schedule*.

"The plot thickens," said Natalie.

"If it gets any thicker, they'll have to add water."

A sound by the door made us look up.

She was tough and leathery, lean and gray. Her wings ended in claws. Her pug nose looked like it smelled something bad.

And that something was us.

"What are you doing in my desk?" she snarled.

It was Ms. Darkwing. The old bat.

My tail twitched. "Uh, looking for background information," I said. "We're from the school newspaper."

Ms. Darkwing frowned. She scuttled up to the desk faster than I thought an old bat could move. *Riiip!* She snatched the paper from my hands.

"Give me that," she said. "What have you seen?"

"Not much," I said. "We just got here."

"Yeah," said Natalie. "We thought you'd make a great story for the newspaper."

Ms. Darkwing rapped Natalie on the beak with a twisted claw.

"You've got a regular nose for news, eh?" she sneered at us. "Well, you won't get any from me, you snoopy kids."

We backed up a couple steps. She followed.

"Aw, please tell us about yourself," I said. "All your fans want to know how you keep your claws so sharp and your desk so neat."

"Let 'em guess," she said. "And as for you, I think I'll tell the principal about you."

"Mr. Zero?" said Natalie. "Do you know him well?"

"Well enough," she said. "And we're going to go see him right now."

Ms. Darkwing stretched her claws toward us. I backed up and bumped into Natalie. My pocket thumped heavily against my leg.

"You think Principal Zero will take your word over ours?" I said, reaching into my pocket. "Don't be such a sap!"

I tossed the weapon at her face. Ms. Darkwing swatted it away and stumbled back, off balance.

"Run, Natalie!"

We shot through the doorway like a spitwad through a straw. Natalie flapped and I dashed. We didn't stop until we'd reached the shelter of the gym.

"That was close," said Natalie.

"Too close . . . for comfort," I said, panting. "But at least . . . we know who's . . . in on this plot."

"We know a lot more than that, Chet. Didn't you see that list?"

"Yeah, it was a lot . . . easier to read this time. Mr. Zero's handwriting . . . is the worst."

Natalie sighed. "Don't you get it? That list tells us what they're up to."

"Oh yeah?" I said. "And what's that?"

"Think about what we've learned," said Natalie. Her tail feathers bobbed as she paced. "Number one, someone kidnapped Principal Zero and substituted a phony."

I picked it up. "Number two, the principal is looking for students who don't think crime is wrong."

"Number three, we saw plans for a vocational school and class schedules."

I frowned. Math has never been my best subject. "And numbers one plus two plus three equal? . . ." I said.

"Come on, Chet! That bogus Principal Zero and his gang are turning Emerson Hicky into a school for crooks!"

## 12

## Hail, Hail, the Gangster's Here

The bell rang, ending recess. It rattled my brain, but not as much as Natalie's idea had.

"Emerson Hicky, a school for crooks?" I said. "But how can that be?"

"Look at it, Chet. Everything fits. The boxes of brass knuckles..."

"The criminals who started working here...," I said.

"The classes in stealing and lying..."

My eyes widened. "Soccer blue!" I said. "You're right."

"'Soccer blue'?" said Natalie.

"It's French—but never mind that. What do we do about these crooks?"

Natalie hopped from foot to foot. "Chet, there's only one thing to do. We've got to tell a teacher."

"What?!"

"We need help," she said. "We can't stop them alone."

"Oh, great." I grabbed my hat and bopped it against my leg as I paced beside the gym.

"It's not bad enough that I've got a partner who's a dame," I muttered. "Now she wants me to turn wimpy and ask a teacher to help solve the case? I'll be laughed out of private-eye society."

Natalie grabbed me by my lapels and shook me.

"Easy, this fabric wrinkles," I said.

"Chet, if you don't tell a teacher, I will," said Natalie. "These crooks are too tough for us."

I glared at her. She glared right back. These stubborn birds. I waited, to let her steam awhile.

"Oh . . . okay," I said. "We'll tell Mr. Ratnose. But if he doesn't believe it, we handle the rest of the case alone. Deal?"

"Deal. Let's tell him at lunch. I'll come to your room."

We went to our classrooms. I sat at my desk, staring at the blackboard. As the minutes crawled by, I could hardly keep my mind on my lessons.

Of course, that's not all that unusual.

At last the lunch bell rang. I hoped our meeting

with Mr. Ratnose wouldn't take long. I mean, saving the school is all well and good, but a guy's got to eat.

The classroom cleared like a nostril after a supersonic sneeze. I dawdled at my desk. Mr. Ratnose looked at me curiously. His whiskers twitched.

"Something wrong, Chet?" he said.

"Why?"

"Usually you're the first one out the door at lunchtime."

"Well...," I said, stalling.

Natalie hustled through the doorway.

"Mr. Ratnose, Natalie and I have something very serious to tell you."

She joined me by his desk. Together we told Mr. Ratnose what we'd seen: Principal Zero's strange behavior, the new criminals at school, the weapons, and the list.

"So you see," I said, "what we've got here is a school full of crooks."

Mr. Ratnose smiled and nodded. "Yep, that's what I've been saying for years," he said.

"No, you don't understand," said Natalie. "This fake principal and his gang are trying to turn the students into criminals, too."

"If you ask me," said Mr. Ratnose, "they're too late."

My stomach knotted and jerked, like a python swallowing a sofa. "Too late?" I said.

"Yep," said Mr. Ratnose. His long nose wrinkled in disapproval. "You kids are already the biggest pack of criminals I've ever seen."

"What?" said Natalie.

"You don't do homework," said Mr. Ratnose, "you write graffiti on the desks, you have no school spirit—in my book, that's criminal behavior."

"But—" I said.

"No *buts,* Mr. Buttinsky. Off with you." Mr. Ratnose marched us to the door. "And stop interrupting my lunch to tell me things I already know."

Natalie followed me out. Mr. Ratnose locked the door, muttering, "Bunch of juvenile delinquents." When he had gone, I turned to Natalie.

"Satisfied?" I said. "Now can we solve this my way?"

She shrugged. "I guess we'll have to. So, what next? Do we—"

*Boing!*

Natalie and I sprawled face-first on the concrete. I rolled over to greet our attacker.

"Hi, hi, hi, you guys!"

It was Popper, the bouncing tree frog. "Hey, hey, it's lunchtime. Let's play!" she squealed.

"Not now, half-pint," I said. "We're on a case."

"Oh, please, please, please. You guys are the only, the only friends I have here."

"I wonder why," I said.

Natalie swatted me. "Sure, we'll play with you," she said. "How about hide-and-seek? You cover your eyes and count to a hundred, then come looking for us."

I had to hand it to her—the bird was devious.

"Okey-dokey-dokey," said Popper. She hid her eyes in the crook of an elbow and started counting. "One-one-one...two-two-two..."

At that rate, it would take her all day to finish. Natalie and I rushed down the hall.

"Sometimes—just sometimes," I said, "I'm glad to have a partner like you." I punched her shoulder.

"Enough mushy stuff," she said.

"Okay, here's the plan: After we eat, we spend the rest of lunch hour looking for the real Principal Zero. They must have him under wraps somewhere."

"Why wait until after we eat?" said Natalie.

I gave her my best steely-eyed look. "Because, birdie, today they've got wolf-spider pizza with extra cheese."

"Lead on, tough guy," she said.

## 13

## Kitty Cornered

We knew that Ms. Darkwing would be looking for us, so Natalie and I kept a low profile. Our search meandered through storerooms and empty classrooms, from the library to the gym.

We turned up zilch. If the crooks had stowed Principal Zero on campus, he was better hidden than a truant officer's heart.

That left Plan B.

Unfortunately, we didn't have a Plan B.

After school, I snagged my skateboard from its hiding place. Natalie and I met on the playground.

She cocked her head. "So," she said, "what's next, Mr. I-Can-Do-It-Alone? Do we just walk into the PTA meeting and tell them what we told Mr. Ratnose? That should go over nicely."

"I'm thinking."

We sat in the shade of the scrofulous tree and tossed around some ideas.

The PTA meeting was at five o'clock. We had to dig up some hard proof by then. Otherwise the PTA would laugh us out of the meeting, and the crooks would win.

Not a cheerful thought. Maybe we could transfer to another school.

At the far end of the playground, a green-and-yellow tree frog was searching among barrels and forts in the sandbox. Pretty persistent, that Popper.

Just then I glanced toward the buildings and saw the principal locking up his office. *Hmm.*

I elbowed Natalie. "Hey, there he goes," I said. "Let's follow him home. Maybe they've got the real Principal Zero stashed at his house."

"Good thinking, private eye," she said.

We edged closer to the bushes and sneaked toward the sidewalk. Soon the fake principal waddled by. His tail waved jauntily, like a bully with your lunch money in his pocket.

"Now we've got him," I whispered.

The bogus principal strolled down the street. We followed. He turned the corner, got behind the wheel of a blue sedan, and drove off.

Rats. It's hard to be a hot-shot private eye when you can't drive yet.

"After him, Natalie!" I said. "I'll come as quick as I can."

She flapped her wings and flew after the car. I jumped on my skateboard and pushed it as fast as I could. After three blocks, I lost sight of both car and bird. I also lost my breath. I panted and waited.

In a couple of minutes, a flutter of wings announced my partner.

"What's keeping you?" said Natalie.

"I'm planning strategy, that's all."

She flew circles around me. "Well, his house isn't far. Come on, I'll lead you there."

A right turn, a left, another right, and there we were. Natalie and I crouched behind some bushes at the foot of a long driveway. At the top sat the blue car. Beyond it, a wide two-story house squatted amidst the trees like a fat toad full of secrets.

Coils of barbed wire surrounded the house, except for the driveway. Spikes decorated the rooftop. Scorched craters in the yard made it look like someone had been playing catch with hand grenades.

"Wow," I said. "Why didn't they just hang a sign that says CAUTION—BAD GUYS AT WORK?"

"Shhh," said Natalie. "Come on, let's take a closer look."

A neighbor lady was watching us from her window. She shook her head in warning, but we just ignored her.

Private eyes don't live by the rules.

Moving slower than a parent-teacher conference, we sneaked up the driveway, past the barbed wire, and through the bushes. Every time a twig cracked, we froze.

Finally we ducked under the windows. Rising carefully to our feet, Natalie and I peeked through the glass.

Inside, the broad back of Principal Zero passed before us. He took off his coat and tie, and tossed them onto the sofa. Then he sat down. From where we watched, we could hear the sofa springs complaining.

Principal Zero reached up with both hands as if to grab his collar. But he grabbed his neck instead. In one move, he peeled back the skin, pulling it up over his chin and face. It was more disgusting than watching the Invisible Man digest a four-course lunch, but I couldn't look away.

Finally the fake principal laid it down. A mask! His rough face split in a smile. This guy could give ugly lessons to a warthog. He obviously wasn't our principal.

But who the heck was he?

# 14

## *F* Is for Fake

"Who the heck is that?" whispered Natalie.

"Just what I was wondering," I said. We pressed our faces nearer to the window.

*Brrring!*

A phone rang on the table before us. If I'd had hair, it would have stood on end.

"Down!" I hissed.

Natalie and I collapsed against the house like a cheap umbrella in a hurricane. Inside, we could hear the big crook talking.

"Yeah," he said. "Come on over. Everything's set. What? Don't worry about those kids. They don't suspect a thing."

Natalie and I exchanged a look.

"Yeah," he continued, "those poor suckers at the meeting won't have a clue. We've got this locked up, I tell you."

The crook chuckled deep in his chest. It sounded like an alligator digesting a handbag salesman.

He hung up. Footsteps clomped, and the sofa complained again. Whoever he was, he didn't have to wear a fake gut to impersonate Mr. Zero. This was one fat cat.

"Okay," I whispered to Natalie. "Let's case this joint. He's got our principal stashed somewhere."

Natalie pussyfooted along the side of the house, peeking into the windows on the first floor. I climbed to the second floor. In my line of work, it pays to be a wall-crawling lizard.

I peered into the rooms. Nothing in the first. Nothing in the second but a pile of old boxes. But when I reached the third window—bingo!

His huge body was wrapped in ropes, and his mouth was taped shut. Principal Zero looked like he'd taken a hayride with a Gila monster and come out on the bottom.

But it was really him. I could tell by his scowl—dark enough to make a werewolf whimper.

"Natalie!" I whispered as loud as I could. She kept staring through a downstairs window.

"Natalie!" I whispered again. She still didn't hear.

"Look, a worm!"

That time she heard. When Natalie glanced up, I pointed at the window and motioned for her to join me. She flapped up to a nearby branch and looked inside.

"That's no worm," she said. "You lied."

"Sorry. Help me get the window open."

We boosted the window and slipped inside. Principal Zero's eyes widened when he saw us. I peeled the tape off his mouth.

"Took you long enough," said Mr. Zero. His whiskers bristled.

Yep. That was our principal, all right.

"What do you mean?" I said. "It took some hard work to find you."

"I knew you'd come," he said. "When that impostor, Knuckles McGee, asked how to act like me, I told him to be nice to you. I knew that would tip you off, and you'd come nosing around."

I had to hand it to him. Principal Zero knew his students.

"Are you all right?" asked Natalie.

"There's no time for tea and sympathy," he said. "Get me out of these ropes. We've got a school to save."

Natalie and I struggled with the knots. It looked like they'd been tied by a tribe of evil Boy Scouts in a bad mood. After what seemed like a century, we freed his legs.

"This is taking too long," said Principal Zero. "Find something sharp and cut these ropes."

We rummaged through the room. No scissors, no saws.

I heard a creak. The door swung open. There stood Ms. Darkwing with a gleaming knife in her hand.

"Looking for one of these?" she said.

# 15

## All Tied Up and No Place to Go

**M**s. Darkwing swung her knife like a ninja chef at a seven-course dinner. She knew how to use it.

Our eyes locked. She sneered. I sneered back. We each stepped forward.

Then I heard it: a faint buzzing above us. I spared a quick glance. A fat, juicy fly was circling lazily.

Ms. Darkwing saw it, too. Her mouth twitched; saliva dribbled from the corner. Just as she opened up to make her move, I shot out my tongue and nabbed the fly.

Bull's-eye.

Even on her best day, no bat can beat a quick-draw gecko when there's food at stake.

Ms. Darkwing snarled. "Smooth move, Gecko.

Now let's see if you're fast enough to beat my friends."

Suddenly the doorway behind her filled with a tough armadillo and a huge, evil cat.

Squint and Knuckles. Sounded like a good name for a comedy team. But somehow I didn't think I'd like their jokes.

"Tie 'em up," said Knuckles.

"Why is it crooks always want to tie me up?" I said. "It's getting boring. Can't you guys think of anything original?"

They exchanged puzzled looks. Natalie and I bolted for the open window. We would have made it, too, if it hadn't been for that old bat. She was fast.

Ms. Darkwing clutched our tails in her claws. That stopped us long enough for Squint to drag us back into the room.

Knuckles and Ms. Darkwing tied up Principal Zero's feet again while Squint pinned one of us under each arm. His armpits smelled worse than a skunk's T-shirt after two weeks in the laundry hamper.

"You won't get away with this!" said our principal. "You *mmph*—"

Knuckles jammed the tape over Mr. Zero's mouth. "Oh, yes, we will," he said. "And you'll be our biggest supporters."

"Never!" I said as they wrapped me in ropes like

a sausage in string. Natalie pecked Ms. Darkwing, who shrieked in pain like an opera mouse butchering the score from *Carmen*.

"We'll never help you," said Natalie. Ms. Darkwing tightened her ropes sadistically.

"Oh, I think you will," said Knuckles, "when we pour the concrete for the new buildings at our Vocational Criminal School. Lying there in the foundation, you'll provide such great support."

He was slimier than a dingo's drool cup. Knuckles chortled nastily. His gang joined him. I would have tossed off a snappy comeback, but they had taped my mouth shut.

"What, no more wisecracks?" said Knuckles. "Well, toodle-oo, kiddies. We have a big meeting to prepare for."

They left, deadbolting the door behind them. We lay there like three lumps of lasagna. *Mmm, lasagna.* I wondered if they would feed us dinner before they buried us in concrete.

I rolled over to face the window. It wasn't far. I crawled for it as fast as I could, like an ancient inchworm with arthritis. If I could just pull myself up, maybe a neighbor would see.

Maybe they'd come investigate.

And maybe we'd starve to death first.

It took forever to reach the wall. Empires rose

and fell. A whole new TV season came and went as I crawled. I heard a door slam below and a car engine start.

The crooks were leaving! If we didn't show up at that meeting, they'd trick the PTA into approving their plan.

I struggled to a sitting position. Natalie and Principal Zero cheered me on with their eyes.

At least I think they did. They could've been swearing, for all I knew.

I levered and twisted my rope-wrapped body upright, like a mummy dancing hip-hop. Finally I stood and leaned on the windowsill. I poked my head outside.

"Hey, hey, hey, I found you!"

I looked down. Popper the tree frog bounced merrily on the ground below. "Now you're it, you're it!" she said. "Or do I have to come up and tag you, tag you first?"

# 16

## Cops and Froggers

"Wowie, wow, wow!" said Popper. She hopped in a circle as she shouted up at me. "You guys are *good* at hide-and-seek. I never would have found you without that nice, nice neighbor lady."

"*Mmph, vvmm, gmff,*" I said. The tape over my mouth didn't help my diction any. I motioned with my head for Popper to come upstairs.

"I have to come up and tag, tag, tag you?" she said. "Okey-dokey-dokey!"

Two short hops and a long leap later, Popper crawled along a tree branch and in through the window. I slid over to make room for her.

She tagged all three of us. "You're it, it, it!"

Then she started back out the window.

"MMMMPH!" Natalie, Principal Zero, and I screamed together.

Popper turned. "What, what? You'll have to speak uppity-up." Finally she noticed the ropes around our bodies and the tape over our mouths.

"Oh," she said. "What a funny, funny game. Can I play, can I please play?"

The little tree frog peeled the tape off Natalie's beak.

"It's no game," said Natalie. "These crooks tied us up and they're trying to take over our school. Untie us, quick. We've got to stop them!"

"Oh boy, oh boy, oh boy," said Popper. "What a fun, fun game—cops and robbers!"

"Mmph!" I said. I'd straighten her out after we were free. She gave me a big-brother sort of feeling. The kind I get when I want to cream my little sister, Pinky.

For a frog, Popper had clever fingers. She untied us all in less time than it takes to sing "Polly Wolly Doodle" backward.

As soon as he was free, Principal Zero started making plans.

"I'll fetch the police," he said. "Chet, Natalie,

you go to the PTA meeting and stall them until we get there."

"What about me, me, me?" said Popper. She quivered like a tuning fork.

"You come with us," said Natalie.

My stomach rumbled. It was long past snack time. "But, Principal Zero," I said, "why do you need us at the meeting? Can't the cops handle this? After all, they've got these crooks dead to rights for the kidnapping and for doing away with Mrs. Shrewer."

His tail twitched. Mr. Zero frowned. "She's just hiding," he said. "Look, you don't understand. I'm not worried about the criminals, I'm worried about the PTA. Once they vote on something, they never change their minds."

Natalie cocked her head. "Oh," she said. "You mean—"

"Exactly," he said. "You've got to keep them from voting on Knuckles McGee's plan, or it's curtains for Emerson Hicky."

And he wasn't talking about interior decorating.

We dashed downstairs. Principal Zero waddled. He tried using the phone, but the crooks had disconnected it. Spoilsports. They weren't as dumb as they looked.

Principal Zero growled. "I'll call from next door. The police can pick me up. You get over to that meeting, pronto!"

We didn't need to hear it again. Natalie, Popper, and I burst out the front door and down the driveway.

"Natalie," I said. "Take me on your back. We've got to fly over there."

"Me too, me too!" said Popper. She hopped like a jumping bean on springs.

"What do I look like," said Natalie, "a passenger pigeon? There's no way I'm letting you two on my back."

"Oh, all right," I said. Then my mental flashbulb went off. "Hey, stop the presses—I've got a great idea!"

"*Hmph,*" said Natalie. "Beginner's luck."

I stood on my skateboard and lifted Popper onto my shoulders. I gripped her ankles tightly.

"Popper, grab Natalie's feet. Natalie, just grab back and flap away. You can tow us there, like water-skiing!"

Natalie sighed and shook her head. "Chet, you've been watching too much TV. But...okay. Let's do it."

She flapped a couple of times for altitude, then

grabbed Popper's hands. And away we went. Faster and faster we rolled. I didn't know if the principal's plan would work.

But I knew one thing.

If we didn't make that meeting on time, at least we'd make it big on *The Wild World of Sports*.

# 17

## Pandemonium at the PTA

**W**ind whipped my coat and lifted my hat. We took a corner on two wheels.

"Yee-haw!" I cried, like a Texas detective.

"Urk!" Popper seconded.

Solo skateboarding would never be the same again.

Heading into the last stretch, Natalie was gasping like a weaselly sixth grader trying a cigarette. Popper was stretched out like a torture victim on the rack.

And me? I was ready for action.

"Faster, faster!" I said. "Get the lead out!"

Natalie flashed me a dirty look. "You try towing...a lard bucket and a pipsqueak...see how fast...you can go," she said between pants.

Dames. They get so moody sometimes.

We rolled into the school parking lot. The auditorium waited just ahead. So did the curb.

"Natalie, there's a—"

*Ba-gonk!*

There was no time to react. My skateboard rammed the curb. The impact jerked Popper's legs from my hands. She and Natalie hit the grass in a tangle of feathers and webbed feet.

Like a slow-motion movie, I watched myself tumble through the air. Unfortunately, things sped up as I landed—*whomp!*—right on top of them.

When the world stopped spinning like a windup

ballerina, I staggered to my feet. Natalie and Popper didn't stir.

"Stop lollygagging around, you guys," I said. "Let's go!"

They groaned. These junior detectives—always lying about on the job.

I rushed through the auditorium doors. In rows of folding chairs sat parents, teachers, and the odd student who couldn't get out of coming. At the front stood the phony Principal Zero. Behind him sat Clint Squint and Ms. Darkwing.

The principal was talking. "So, as you can see," he said, "this vocational school will be good for the students, good for the community, and good for Emerson Hicky Elementary."

The audience swallowed his line like a catfish gulps mosquito fudge ripple ice cream. They applauded politely.

Principal Zero—or should I say, Principal Knuckles—smiled like a dentist facing a mouthful of expensive cavities. His gang looked tickled, too. If you've never seen an armadillo and a bat grin, take it from me: It's not a pretty sight.

"Now, if there are no questions," he said, "let's put this matter to a vote. All in favor—"

"Wait!" I said. "I have a question."

I ducked behind a parent, so Knuckles couldn't spot me.

"Yes, someone in the back?" He shaded his eyes and peered into the audience.

"Here's my question: How do you define *vocational*?"

The fake principal's tail twitched. He snapped, "Who said that?" Then he caught himself and forced a chuckle that sounded as merry as a rattlesnake with the mumps.

"Well," said Knuckles, "it means, 'relating to training for a job or career.' We'll train these children for a nice, profitable career."

"What kind of career is that?" I said. I crept down the row.

Knuckles tracked me with his eyes. He signaled someone behind me. I turned, and Guido the janitor trotted toward me with arms spread wide.

"We'll train these children for careers in a growth industry," said the bogus principal. "Any other questions?"

I left my row of chairs and scooted down the aisle. With Guido on my tail, I had no time to talk.

"I'd like to know something," said a voice from the back. "What kind of growth industry makes kids take classes in stealing cars and picking pockets?"

Good old Natalie, right on cue.

The audience murmured. "What's this about stealing cars?" said a dignified old pigeon. "Whatever does she mean?"

"She means they want to turn this into a school for crooks!" I shouted.

Guido grabbed at me. I ducked under his arms and almost got knocked out by his B.O. Didn't any of these criminals know about personal hygiene? They needed to take Marge Supial's "Healthy Habits" class.

I jumped to the wall and scuttled out of reach. Mr. Squint started down the aisle for Natalie.

"Pay no attention to these kids," Knuckles growled. "They're just playing a childish prank. Let's vote. All in favor—"

The audience rumbled like a pack of wolverines who forgot to make dinner reservations. An argument broke out between two parents. Jabbering teachers converged on Knuckles.

I leaped off the wall and onto the stage. Dodging behind chairs, I dashed for the fake principal, with Guido in hot pursuit. If only I could rip off that mask...

I hopped onto Knuckles's back like a flea on an elephant.

"He's a fake!" I cried. "Look!"

I tugged with both hands at the mask. Knuckles's big paws clamped down on my wrists.

"Somebody get this gecko off me," he snarled.

Guido plucked me off like a piece of belly-button lint. I looked for Natalie, but Mr. Squint had her cornered.

It looked like our luck had run out.

Bye-bye, detectives, hello crime school.

# 18

## Knuckles's Sandwich

Popper burst through the back door. "It's a raid, it's a raid!" she cried.

Blue uniforms poured into the auditorium from all sides. Parents screamed. Teachers shouted. I bit Guido's paw.

"Yow!" He dropped me like a bad habit.

The crooks made a break for the door by the stage. Too late! Cops surrounded them.

*Fweeeet!*

Principal Zero's whistle cut through the pandemonium like a belch through a church service. Everyone fell silent. He waddled up the aisle toward me.

"Took you long enough," I said.

"Principals don't run," he said. Mr. Zero turned to the cops. "Officers, arrest these evildoers."

The police looked from the fake principal to the real one. They hesitated.

"Arrest this man for disrupting our meeting!" said Knuckles.

Principal Zero advanced on him, eyes narrowed and neck fur bristling.

"It's not just that you're guilty of kidnapping, assault, and plotting to do very bad things...," he said. In one quick move, our principal reached out and tore off the mask. "But you're impersonating a principal, mister, and I won't stand for that!"

The parents and teachers gasped at the unmasked Knuckles McGee. I didn't blame them. If ugliness were art, he'd have been the Moan-a Lisa.

Principal Zero wound up like King Kong pitching for the World Series. His punch connected with a *whump* that made me wince. The criminal went down like a concrete submarine.

"Enjoy your knuckle sandwich...Knuckles," purred Mr. Zero. He smoothed his whiskers and turned to the cops. "Take them away."

I heard a heavy sigh. There, just behind me, slumped a dejected Rocky Rhode, horned toad and juvenile delinquent.

"Oh, man, this is the pits," she said. "I knew

it was too good to be true—a principal who really understood me."

"Don't worry," I said. "I think the real Principal Zero understands you, too."

Rocky grumped. "I know. That's the problem."

The police loaded the four crooks into a paddy wagon outside, while Principal Zero told the crowd what had happened. Popper watched everything, wide-eyed and twitching.

"Wowie, wow, wow!" she said. "This is the best, the best cops-and-robbers game ever!"

Natalie joined me by the door. She groomed her feathers as we watched the police van pull away.

"Just think," I said. "We never would have uncovered this plot if I wasn't such a great artist."

"Yeah, right," she said. "Chet, you can barely draw a bath."

I told you: Great artists are never appreciated.

Principal Zero spotted us and stepped away from the crowd. His heavy paw landed on my shoulder. He squeezed. I flinched.

"You kids have done great work on this case," he said. "Take some time off. You deserve it."

"Gee, thanks," I said.

He smiled. "Let's see . . . today is Friday. Don't come back to school until Monday."

He wasn't funny. But he was our principal.

As Natalie and I walked away, I began planning my next cartoon.

I'd start with a big, fat Principal Zero. And for the sake of Art, I'd make his stomach bigger than a Thanksgiving Day parade float....

*Mmm, Thanksgiving...* That reminded me of dinner. Art could wait. I'd find my next masterpiece at home on a plate.

# What's Eating Chet?
# Find Out in
# *Farewell, My Lunchbag*

Mrs. Bagoong is a hundred pounds of tough, leathery iguana. Her eyes are like chocolate drops, her cheeks soft as AstroTurf, and about the same color. Her thick, powerful body is wrapped in a blue apron that says KISS THE COOK.

Yuck. Nobody in his right mind would try to smooch Mrs. Bagoong.

"What's up, brown eyes?" I said. "If your face were any longer, you'd have to rent an extra chin."

Mrs. Bagoong sighed. "Chet, honey," she said, "we've got problems."

My heart raced faster. "You're not running out of mothloaf, are you?"

"Not yet."

I relaxed. "So it's not serious, then."

"Serious enough," she said. "Someone's stealing our food."

Mrs. Bagoong sunk her face in her hands. She looked sadder than a wilted bowl of broccoli on a muggy day.

One thick, iguanoid tear slithered down her cheek. "If I can't stop this, I don't know what will happen. They might close the cafeteria, or even fire me."

The tear did it. I can't stand to see a reptile cry.

"All right, enough of that," I said. "Chet Gecko is on the case. Food thieves, beware!"

She cracked a tiny smile and sniffled. I swaggered to the door and flung it open. I saluted her.

"See ya *mañana,* iguana."

*Ba-whonk!*

I walked into a stack of cans.

"Uh, Chet, honey? That's the pantry."

Another great exit, ruined.

## Be on the lookout for more mysteries from the Tattered Casebook of Chet Gecko

**Case #1**  *The Chameleon Wore Chartreuse*

Some cases start rough, some cases start easy. This one started with a dame. (That's what we private eyes call a girl.) She was cute and green and scaly. She looked like trouble and smelled like . . . grasshoppers.

Shirley Chameleon came to me when her little brother, Billy, turned up missing. (I suspect she also came to spread cooties, but that's another story.) She turned on the tears. She promised me some stinkbug pie. I said I'd find the brat.

But when his trail led to a certain stinky-breathed, bad-tempered, jumbo-sized Gila monster, I thought I'd bitten off more than I could chew. Worse, I had to chew fast: If I didn't find Billy in time, it would be bye-bye, stinkbug pie.

**Case #4**  *The Big Nap*

My grades were lower than a salamander's slippers, and my bank account was trying to crawl under a duck's belly. So why did I take a case that didn't pay anything?

Put it this way: Would *you* stand by and watch some evil power turn *your* classmates into hypnotized zombies? (If that wasn't just what normally happened to them in math class, I mean.)

My investigations revealed a plot meaner than a roomful of rhinos with diaper rash.

Someone at Emerson Hicky was using a sinister video game to put more and more students into la-la-land. And it was up to me to stop it, pronto—before that someone caught up with me, and I found myself taking the Big Nap.

## Case #5  *The Hamster of the Baskervilles*

Elementary school is a wild place. But this was ridiculous.

Someone—or some*thing*—was tearing up Emerson Hicky. Classrooms were trashed. Walls were gnawed. Mysterious tunnels riddled the playground like worm chunks in a pan of earthworm lasagna.

But nobody could spot the culprit, let alone catch him.

I don't believe in the supernatural. My idea of voo-doo is my mom's cockroach ripple ice cream.

Then a teacher reported seeing a monster on full-moon night, and I got the call.

At the end of a twisted trail of clues, I had to answer the burning question: Was it a vicious, supernatural were-hamster on the loose, or just another Science Fair project gone wrong?

## Case #6  *This Gum for Hire*

Never thought I'd see the day when one of my worst enemies would hire me for a case. Herman the Gila Monster was a sixth-grade hoodlum with a first-rate left hook. He told me someone was disappearing the football team, and he had to put a stop to it. Big whoop.

He told me he was being blamed for the kidnappings, and he had to clear his name. Boo hoo.

Then he said that I could either take the case and earn a nice reward, or have my face rearranged like a bargain-basement Picasso painted by a spastic chimp.

I took the case.

But before I could find the kidnapper, I had to go undercover. And that meant facing something that scared me worse than a chorus line of criminals in steel-toed boots: P.E. class.